An D1589143 *n*

Septimouse
and the
Cheese Party

Illustrated by

Kav Widdowson

HAPPY CAT BOOKS

Published by Happy Cat Books Ltd.
Bradfield, Essex CO11 2UT, UK

First published 2004
1 3 5 7 9 10 8 6 4 2

A CIP catalogue record for this book is available from the British Library

ISBN 1 903285 70 4

Printed in Poland

Contents

1

Invitations

"I won!" yelled Septimouse as Katie took him out of her pocket and put him down on the kitchen table. "Me and my mouse cheese won the Cheese of the Year Prize. Whoopee!" and he did five cartwheels.

"Congratulations, Septimouse," said Mum. "Your cheese certainly deserved to win."

"Of course it did," shouted the mouse

leaping up and down with excitement. "Am I not the greatest mouse the world has ever known? Of course my cheese deserved to win."

"Calm down, Septimouse," said Dad. "I know this has been an important day in your life, but you are getting over-excited."

At that moment the phone rang. Mum answered.

"It's the editor of *The Cheesemaker's Monthly*," she whispered. "They want to interview us about our, eh, I mean Septimouse's winning cheese."

"Umm, eh, let's eh, take it in the other room," said Dad and they rushed out.

"It's MY cheese that won the competition," said Septimouse, with a tear running down his cheek, "but big, big person Mum and big, big person Dad are getting all the credit and it's not fair."

Katie took a tissue out of the box and tore

off a tiny bit and gave it to Septimouse. The
mouse dried his tears and sniffed sadly.

"I agree with you, Septimouse," said Katie
sympathetically. "It's not fair. You and your
family make the cheese in your cheese
factory under this house and when they do
well, we humans get the praise."

"It is very hard to bear, little big person

Katie," agreed the mouse. "Very hard indeed. You see, I would so love to be in the papers and on television and be as famous as I deserve to be."

"But, Septimouse, we have to keep you a secret," Katie pointed out. "I mean, if people knew that your wonderful 4S cheese was made by a family of mice and that you then blow it up and make it huge, well no one would buy it."

"Are you sure about that, little big person?"

"Well, people are rather silly about mice, Septimouse, and I think that if they knew the truth about your cheese they wouldn't buy it."

"Oh dear," sighed Septimouse. "The big, big people are very silly sometimes but I suppose you are right. Even I, the seventh son of a seventh son and endowed with amazing magical powers, can see no way round the oddness of big, big people."

"I think you should hold a wonderful party to celebrate winning the Cheese of the Year Prize," said Katie.

"There's no point," wept Septimouse. "If you had a big, big persons' party, I and my family couldn't come and join in because I am a big secret. You would all be pretending that big, big person Mum and big, big person Dad had made the cheese. No, that idea doesn't tempt me one bit."

"No, I meant a mouse party."

"We mice already had a party when the cheese factory opened, so why have another one?"

"Because there can never be too many parties and you have something new to celebrate now."

"But my family already know that I am wonderful," said Septimouse sadly. "I want my fame to spread beyond my mouse hole and this house."

"But Septimouse, think how lovely it would be for your mother and father and John, James, Julius, Joseph, Jeremy and Jack to have a celebration. Think how hard they have all worked producing enough 4S cheese to meet the demand of all the big, big people who want to buy it."

"I suppose so," sighed Septimouse. "You are quite right, little big person Katie, I am being selfish. For my family this is a big day and I should put aside my feelings of sadness and get a party organised for them."

At that moment Mum and Dad came back into the room.

"Septimouse is a bit upset," Katie told them, "because you are getting all the fuss and attention over the cheese."

"I don't blame you for being upset," cried Dad. "I wish there was something I could do about it. I just don't know how we can make it up to you, Septimouse."

"Sir!" cried the mouse, "I have an idea. Little big person Katie wants me to have a mouse party for my family to celebrate the Cheese of the Year Award. Now if you could buy the biggest selection of cheeses you could get and bring them here, then we really would have the greatest mouse cheese party of all times. Now that would be something! Septimouse the Great scores again. Off you go and get me the cheeses and I'll go and organise the mice."

A few hours later, Septimouse stuck his head out of his mouse hole and called out, "Little big person Katie, come here and collect your invitations to my mouse celebration."

Katie knelt down and took the tiny invitations from the mouse.

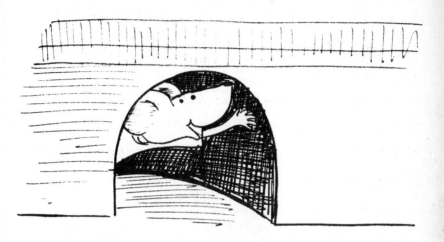

"The writing is so small I can hardly read it," said Katie.

"No problem," replied the mouse, "I will use my incredible skills to make the invitation big person size," and holding his hands out over the invitation and closing his eyes, Septimouse intoned:

> "Invitation neat and small,
> Not meant for people gross and tall.
> Grow into a larger size,
> For I am Septimouse the Wise.

Let the people, little and big,
Come to my party and do a jig.
Invitation grow, grow, grow,
Because I say it shall be so!"

Katie and Septimouse watched the
invitations grow. Katie tried to grab one
but it just continued to grow.

"Do something, Septimouse," cried Katie.
"Look, the invitations are almost touching
the ceiling."

"My magic was too strong," shouted Septimouse. "But fear not, little big person Katie, I will right the wrong:

Invitations from the ceiling fall,
Reduce your size now one and all."

The cards immediately returned to their original size.

"Don't worry about it, Septimouse," said Katie. "You just tell me when we should come to the party, we don't really need invitations."

"Yes, you do!" replied the mouse indignantly. "This is my super important celebration and things are going to be done properly and, what is more, little big person Katie, I am not going to be messed around by three silly invitations. Now, absolute quiet while I concentrate all my seventh son of a seventh son powers on getting this

absolutely right."

Septimouse closed his eyes and sat in the lotus position and after five minutes he chanted:

"Invitations, this won't do.
Septimouse is warning you.
Grow by five times, no more,
And wait for me by the kitchen door."

A moment later the three invitations were sitting by the kitchen door and the right size.

"And about time too," grumbled the mouse.

Katie picked up the three invitations and looked at them.

"Big, big person Dad, big, big person Mum and little big person Katie," she read out. "Can I open mine now?"

"Pray do," replied Septimouse grandly.

Katie read out:

"Septimouse the Great invites you to a Grand Cheese Tasting Party to celebrate his winning the Cheese of the Year Prize at 7 p.m. on Saturday October 12th in the Cheese Factory.   R.S.V.P."

"Oh, Septimouse, I'd love to come, and I'm sure Mum and Dad would too. It's going to be a lovely party."

"Yes it will be, little big person Katie, but I would really prefer to be interviewed on the television and have my picture in the papers.

It is very hard to be so brilliant and only be recognised by mice and cats and dogs."

"And us," reminded Katie.

"Yes, and you, but all the rest think it is people who made my marvellous cheese."

"We would tell them if we could," Katie assured him.

"I know," sniffed the mouse, "but it is very hard anyway."

"Well, think how happy all the mice will be to have the chance to taste all those other cheeses. They'll know that without your very special magic they would never have had that experience, not even in their wildest dreams."

"You have spoken truly, O little big person," said Septimouse wiping his eyes. "Yes, I will give the mice the most exciting mouse experience in the whole wide world."

At that moment Oscar pushed the door open and walked in.

"Hello, Septi old boy," said the cat. "What's going on?"

"Nothing that would interest you, Oscar," Septimouse assured him. "I have won the Cheese of the Year Prize and the mice are having a cheese-tasting party to celebrate."

"Another party!" cried Oscar. "Can I come? I enjoyed the last one. Oh please, Septimouse."

"What's Oscar saying?" asked Katie, who

didn't understand cat language.

"He wants to come to the party too but he can't."

"Why not?" asked Katie.

"Because cats don't like cheese so there's no point," and Septimouse turned back to Oscar and said, "Meow, meeow, meow."

Oscar's face crumpled and he went and curled up in the corner and looked miserable.

"Oh, don't be mean, Septimouse. Oscar

came to the last party. He's your friend."

"I know, Katie, but the mice don't feel comfortable with a cat around and Oscar doesn't have a clue about cheese-tasting. If it was a fish-tasting party, that would be entirely different. As it is he'll just have to accept that this is one party he won't be in on. Now I am going home to organise the party and please ask the big, big people to be here at this time tomorrow to discuss the cheeses with me," and he scampered off to the mouse hole.

Katie went over to Oscar and stroked him.

"Don't take any notice of Septimouse," she told the cat. "He's a bit upset because only the mice know how wonderful he is."

Oscar blinked at her.

"Oh dear," sighed Katie. "Of course, you don't understand what I say and Septimouse isn't here to translate. Poor old Oscar, poor old cat."

2

Preparing the Party

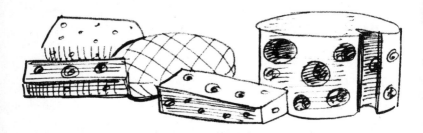

As soon as Septimouse had retreated to the mouse hole, Mum and Dad came in with seventy-five different kinds of cheese.

"Oh, Septimouse will be thrilled to bits when he sees all these cheeses," said Katie.

"I certainly hope so," said Dad. "I feel so uncomfortable about getting all the praise for the 4S cheese. I wish there was a way I could let Septimouse take all the limelight but I just don't see how I can."

"Don't even think about it," said Mum

quickly. "We will do everything we can for Septimouse and his family but we can't let the public know that the 4S cheese is made by mice and is then expanded to fifty times its original size by a mouse who is the seventh son of a seventh son and has magical powers."

"I know," groaned Dad. "I mean, even if

we did come clean, no one would believe us, they'd just think we'd gone mad and in the unlikely event of being taken seriously, well no one would buy the cheese and we'd be broke again."

"Exactly," Mum agreed. "So let's stop worrying about it and put all our energies into helping to make sure that this celebratory party is the best mouse party ever."

"Did I hear something about a mouse party?" came a small voice.

"Ah, Septimouse," said Dad, "there you are. Look, I brought you seventy-five different kinds of cheeses; we have here cheeses from France, Germany, Switzerland, Norway, Denmark, Italy, Greece and Holland."

"Lift me onto the table, someone," cried the mouse. "Let me see these seventy-five different cheeses from so many countries of origin."

Mum lifted him up and Septimouse looked at the cheeses spread out on the table.

"I must try a little of each one, just so that I know what it is I am offering my guests," he explained and he proceeded to nibble away at the cheeses.

"I don't think you should try them all at

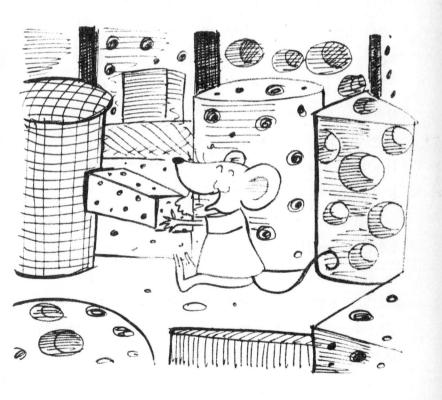

one go," protested Mum. "You'll get sick."

"Nonsense!" replied Septimouse. "If there is one thing mice cannot get too much of it is cheese," and he went on going from cheese to cheese saying, "Oh, yum" or "Super plus delicious" or "How divine" or "Ummm, out of this world."

"So you approve?" said Dad.

"Definitely," replied the mouse. "Now all I have to do is shrink them all, so they can go into the mouse hole and then I can make them grow as much as we need to at the party. Thanks to my amazing magical skills, the mice will have the greatest mouse party ever."

"I think we should keep the cheeses in our fridge until the day of the party," suggested Mum.

"Good idea," agreed the mouse. "So good I'm surprised I didn't think of it myself. Alright big, big person Mum, I will come

out and shrink the cheeses at about five on
Saturday afternoon and I will shrink you
and big, big person Dad and little big
person Katie at the same time, so that you
can join us in our celebration."

"Well, eh, I mean, eh, Septimouse, maybe
this party should just be for mice and we

can have our own separate celebration?"

"Certainly not," cried Septimouse. "How can you even think of such a thing? You three and the inspector are the only people who know about the amazing wonderfulness of me. I want you to come to the party and tell the mice how famous I am and how much the big, big people out there like my cheese. No, you must come, you most certainly must."

"Alright," sighed Dad. "If it's that important to you, we'll come."

So at five o'clock on Saturday evening Mum and Dad and Katie sat in the kitchen dressed in their best party clothes.

"I wish we weren't going," whispered Dad. "I mean, we can't talk to the other mice except for Mr Mouse."

"Shush," whispered Mum back. "It's the least we can do to repay Septimouse for everything he's done for us. We wouldn't

have been able to stay in this house if it
hadn't been for him. We won't stay for long,
but we must be very positive while we are
there, smile a lot and eat a lot of cheese."

"I'm a bit worried," said Katie. "You see,
when Septimouse tried to make the

invitations grow, he kept making mistakes and they grew and grew till they went up to the ceiling."

"Don't tell me," groaned Dad, "I don't want to hear about it. I mean we've got to let him shrink us or we can't go to the party, so let's hope Septimouse was just in bad form with the invitations because he was upset."

"I hope so," agreed Mum. "But it does

make me feel a bit uneasy."

"Uneasy," came a voice. "About what?"

"Oh, hello Septimouse," said Katie. "You're looking very smart in your bow tie."

"You all look good, too, in your best party clothes. Nothing is too good for the great mouse cheese celebration!" replied the mouse. "Now first of all I'll shrink the cheeses. I've got them all ready on the other side to receive them."

"Right," said Mum. "Now do you want to shrink the plates they're on as well?"

"Why not?" said the mouse. "Here goes:

Hear me, hear me, noble plate,
Shrink for Septimouse the Great.
Cheeses from the shopping mall,
Shrink and become mouse small."

Mum and Dad and Katie look at each other and breathed a sigh of relief as the plates

and cheeses shrunk. Mum put the tiny
plates by the mouse hole and they
disappeared inside.

"Now you three stand by the mouse hole
and I'll shrink you," commanded
Septimouse.

So they lined up and Septimouse raised his
hands high and chanted:

"Big people in a trice,
Be small like little mice."

A moment later, the three humans and Septimouse were standing by the mouse hole ready to go in.

"Come on," said Septimouse. "Welcome to my grand celebratory party."

3

Disaster Strikes

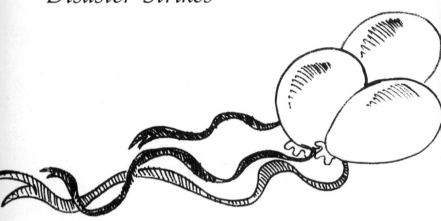

Mum and Dad and Katie stood at the entrance to the mouse hole and felt a bit uncomfortable.

"Come on in," cried Septimouse. "Come on in," and he began to squeak excitedly at the hundreds of mice milling around the mouse hole. Each mouse was nibbling away at a piece of 4S cheese. The mice all smiled at

Mum and Dad and Katie and began to clap appreciatively.

"I've been telling them how none of this would have happened without you," Septimouse told them. "They want you to say a few words."

"Oh dear," mumbled Dad. "I mean, eh, I don't know what to say."

"I'll do the talking then," said Mum. "I'll just tell them about how we would have lost the house if it hadn't been for Septimouse and how the mouse cheese is very, very popular."

"And I'll tell them how wonderful Septimouse is," added Katie.

Septimouse looked modest and smiled, "That is not necessary, little big person Katie, because every mouse here knows that I am super-plus special, but if you feel the need to say it, I would be the last to stop you. But first I must give you all the power of mouse speech, so that they will understand you," and he held up his paws and chanted:

"Big, big people shrunk so small,
Speak to these mice one and all.
Start to squeak like little mice,
I command it in a trice."

"Listen to me," squeaked Mum, "I sound

just like Mrs Mouse. Oh isn't this fun?"

"Think nothing of it," replied Septimouse. "For the seventh son of a seventh son, it was nothing, nothing at all. Now make your speech, the mice are waiting, because until you have spoken the mice can't start eating all these delicious peoply cheeses."

"Ladies and gentlemen, Septimouse and mice," said Mum. "I know how anxious you all are to try the seventy-five different cheeses that we bought for you from the big, big people's shop, so I will be very brief."

The mice all clapped politely.

"All I have to say is that however good these cheeses are, none of them is more delicious than the 4S cheese that Septimouse and his family make and which has just, deservedly, won the Cheese of the Year Prize. Will you please all raise your cheese and join me in a toast to Septimouse, his family and 4S cheese."

All the mice put the paw clutching the cheese in the air and said, "To Septimouse, his family and 4S cheese."

"And I just want to say how special Septimouse is and how without him my family would have been in big trouble and I hope that everyone here knows what a truly wonderful seventh son of a seventh son mouse he is."

Septimouse smiled and nodded in agreement, while all the other mice said, "Hear, hear."

"I want to say something, too," said Katie and she climbed onto a chair. "I want to say that it is very unfair that Septimouse cannot take the credit for the wonderful cheese that is made in this mouse hole. Because people have to think that my mother and father made the cheese, we are getting all the praise and publicity and I think it is very wrong and I want to thank Septimouse for

being so, well, so sporting about it. I know
that Septimouse has found it difficult, so
three cheers for Septimouse. Hip, hip … "

"Hurray!" all the mice joined in, and then
began to sing:

"For he's a jolly good mousey,
For he's a jolly good mousey,

For he's a jolly good mousey,
And so say all of us.

For he's a jolly good mousey,
For he's a jolly good mousey,
For he's a jolly good mousey,
Which nobody can deny."

"Thank you, friend, thank you," yelled
Septimouse. "Now let the cheese tasting
commence!"

The mice began to tuck into the cheeses
and soon squeaks of delight and
appreciation could be heard.

"Here, try this one," Mrs Mouse said to
Katie. "Quickly before it all goes, it is simply
delicious."

"Yes," agreed Mr Mouse, "and have a
nibble of this one with the holes in it. I
never tasted anything as good in my life."

Soon Mum and Dad and Katie were eating

cheese with the mice and enjoying the
cheese tasting as much as anyone.

When every last crumb of cheese had been
eaten, one of the mice said, "Septimouse, Mr
and Mrs Mouse, John, James, Julius, Joseph,
Jeremy, Jack, we would all like to see how
you make the 4S cheese."

"Yes," cried another. "Show us what you
do, we've never seen a cheese factory in
action."

"Show us how the prize-winning cheese is

made," chorused the mice.

Septimouse climbed up onto the side of the big vat and held his hand up for silence.

"Mice, people friends. My family and I will now demonstrate how we make the famous and prize-winning 4S cheese, named of course after me. First of all, this large vat is where the initial process goes on. Now this vat is where we put all the milk that is the basis of all cheesemaking. The vat is, as you can see, very large. From my position here on the edge of the vat I can see how deep and dark it is."

Septimouse put his hand to his head and began to sway from side to side.

"Oh dear, I feel a bit dizzy, a bit sick."

"Stand still," called Katie. "Just stay where you are. I'll come and get you down," and she rushed for the ladder that led to the top of the vat, closely followed by Mr Mouse. Everyone else held their breath and hoped

that help would get to Septimouse in time.
Just as Katie was about to grab the mouse,
Septimouse opened his eyes, gave a groan
and fell into the vat.

"Get me a stepladder quickly," called Mr
Mouse urgently.

"Here, I've got it," cried Katie. "Quick,
over the side with it."

"Septimouse," called Mrs Mouse. "My boy, my son, are you alright? Speak to your mother. Are you hurt?"

There was no reply.

"Don't worry too much," said Mr Mouse fondly to his wife. "He is probably a bit stunned from his fall, nothing serious I'm sure. Come on, Katie, we'd better go and get the little rascal out of the vat."

As soon as the ladder was dangling over the side of the vat, Mr Mouse went down followed by Katie.

"Can we come too?" asked John, James, Julius, Joseph, Jeremy, and Jack.

"You all stay up there," called Mr Mouse.

"Yes," called Katie from deep inside the vat. "We can manage, except that it's very dark in here."

"Grab a candle, everyone who is standing near one," cried Mrs Mouse, "and hold it over the side of the vat."

Instantly there was light enough for Katie and Mr Mouse to see Septimouse lying silent and still on the floor of the vat.

"He's alright, my love," called Mr Mouse. "He's breathing normally, he's just hit his head very hard. He'll be right as rain in a day or two."

"Oh, Septimouse, speak to me, say something. Please say something," said Katie, trying not to cry.

There was no reply.

"Could someone throw down a rope," Mr Mouse shouted. "Then we can lift Septimouse out of here."

The mice pulled Septimouse out of the vat

and soon he was lying in his bed being
lovingly cared for by his mother.

Once everyone was sure that Septimouse
was going to be alright, the guests left.
Only Mum and Dad and Katie were left.

"Maybe we should be going, too," said
Mum, "since there's nothing more we can
do."

"Thank you so much for coming and for bringing all those wonderful cheeses, ummm, my mouth waters at the very thought of them," said Mr Mouse. "I know Septimouse would want me to say a very special thank you."

"Yes, and thank you for your help in saving my boy," said Mrs Mouse, giving Katie a big hug.

"Yes, well, I suppose it is time to become big and little big people again," said Mum.

Then there was a terrible silence.

"But Mum," said Katie, "only Septimouse knows how to make us bigger and smaller."

"Oh no," groaned Dad. "We will have to stay tiny until Septimouse comes round. He's the only one who knows how to enlarge us. What a terrible situation. What a disaster! What are we going to do now?"

4

Joseph's Amazing Run

Mum and Dad and Katie all looked at each other.

"Oh dear," said Dad. "What an awful day this has been. I don't know what to do now."

Katie gave a huge yawn, which she tried to stifle.

"Sorry Dad, but I am so tired."

"Yes, well it is time for bed," smiled Dad.

"Let's try and live our lives as we always have and pretend things are normal. Come on up you go and maybe you'll get lucky and I'll come and read Harry Potter with you."

"That would be great," said Katie, yawning again and she walked out of the mouse hole and into the kitchen followed by her parents. Oscar stood over them, huge and looming.

"Hello old cat," said Katie.

Oscar howled and began to scratch the carpet.

"Stop that," shouted Mum, "you know you're not allowed to do that."

Oscar hissed at her and hit her with his paw. Mum went sprawling.

"Quick, retreat, back into the mouse hole," yelled Dad, and they all raced back as fast as they could leaving Oscar panting at the entrance.

"What's up with Oscar?" questioned Mum, looking troubled. "He's never behaved like that before."

Dad groaned. "I forgot to feed him. The poor creature is starving and he's probably confused as well."

"So what are we going to do now?" demanded Mum. "We can't stay here for ever, we need to get back into our home."

Mr Mouse coughed.

"A suggestion. Why don't we send one of our boys out there to lure the cat out of the cat door, then we can lock it from the inside and we will all be safe. Let me ask Joseph, who is a champion mouse runner, if he would like to volunteer."

Mr Mouse turned and spoke in mouse squeaks to his family. Mrs Mouse burst into tears and clutched her mice children to her. But a very slim mouse with long legs ran to the mouse hole grinning and jumping up and down with excitement.

"Joseph wants to go my love, we must encourage our children to be brave. Off you go my boy and I'm proud of you," cried Mr Mouse, waving his son on.

The mice and Mum and Dad and Katie all stood in the entrance to the mouse hole and yelled:

"Run for it Joseph, run for your life."

The mouse raced across the kitchen like greased lightning and out of the cat flap. Oscar followed close on his heels. Mr Mouse rushed across the room and locked the cat door and they all sat down and breathed a huge sigh of relief. Mrs Mouse climbed up the curtains and looked anxiously out of the window, weeping noisily, then suddenly she stopped and smiled.

"He's alright," she called to her husband. "He just ran back into the house. Three cheers for Joseph!" And she slid down the curtains and gave her husband a hug.

"I think we should phone our friend the Environmental Health Inspector," decided Mum, "since she already knows the truth about Septimouse and the cheese, and get her over here to help."

"Excellent idea," said Dad. Then his face fell. "But we can't reach the phone."

"You'll have to climb up the curtains, like my dear wife, and climb onto the sofa and then sit on the arm of the sofa and talk down the phone," Mr Mouse told them.

So all three of them climbed painfully up the curtains, jumped onto the sofa, walked across it and scrambled onto the arm near the phone. When they got there they were all exhausted.

"Push the phone off its perch," Dad told them. "Come on all together, one, two, three, heave."

At the third go, the phone fell off its perch.

"Right," said Dad, "now we need to look up the number." Mum managed to open the phone book at the right page and told Katie the number.

"Katie, you stand on the key board and bang the numbers with your foot," said her father. "Mum and I are too big to do that."

So Katie danced on the keys till the phone rang. When it was answered, Katie lay down by the mouthpiece and yelled at the top of her voice.

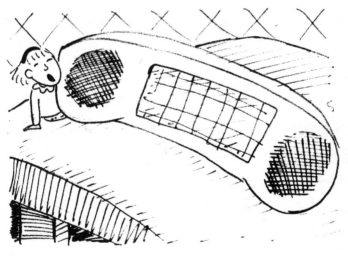

"Hi there, it's Katie, Septimouse's friend."

"Who do you want to speak to?" said a cross voice. "I don't know anyone called Katie or Septimus."

"Sorry," yelled Katie, "I must have dialled the wrong number."

"Yes, well be more careful next time," grumbled the man and slammed the phone down.

"Just try again Katie," said Mum. "Take it slowly and you'll get it right this time."

The phone rang and rang.

"She must be out," sniffed Katie, trying not to cry.

Just then the phone was picked up.

"Hello," said a breathless voice.

"Hello," cried Katie. "This is Katie here, Septimouse's friend."

"Hello Katie," she replied. "How nice to hear from you."

"This is an emergency," Katie shouted.

"Septimouse shrunk us and then he had a fall. He's unconscious and Oscar has been chasing us. Please come over and help. You're our only hope."

"I'll be there, don't worry. Will you be able to let me in? Oh no, of course you won't. Oh dear."

"There's a key under the second flower pot outside the back door," Mum yelled down the phone. "You let yourself in. Make sure Oscar is kept outside and bring some cat food to feed him."

"I'm on my way, you hang on in there. I'll be with as soon as I can. The cavalry is on its way!"

5

The Gentleman of the Press

Mum, Dad, Katie and all the mice lined up on the window sill to look out for the inspector. When the car drew up they all yelled and waved and hugged each other. The Inspector saw them and smiled, and waved a large packet of cat food in the air. Oscar walked round her feet, wailing. Carefully, she put the food in a container and put it down for him. Oscar began to eat greedily. Then the inspector quickly found the key and making sure Oscar was busy, nipped into the house.

"Oh, Inspector, thank goodness you were in," cried Dad.

"Stop calling me inspector, it makes me feel uncomfortable. My name is Suzanne. Now what are we going to do?"

"Maybe Mr Mouse can remember some of Septimouse's spells," suggested Mum.

"I would if I could," said Mr Mouse shaking his head, "but you see I am only a seventh son, not the seventh son of a seventh son, so I alas, have no magical powers."

"Then it looks as though we'll have to wait for Septimouse to come round," said Suzanne. "Where is he by the way?"

"In the mouse hole," Katie told her. "Should we bring him out?"

"Might as well. Then we'll know the minute he comes round."

Dad and Mr Mouse slid down the curtains and ran into the mouse hole and came out a

few minutes later with the unconscious
Septimouse on a stretcher. Suzanne took out
some smelling salts and waved them in front
of Septimouse's nose.

"No response," she sighed. Just then the
front door bell rang loudly.

"Quick," hissed Mum. "Hide behind the
curtains."

Once she had made sure they were all safely out of sight, Suzanne went and opened the door.

"Good morning, Madam," said the man on the doorstep, "I am from the local paper. You, I presume, are Mrs Kingsley of 4S cheese fame."

"Well, eh, no," said Suzanne.

"Ah, now that is unfortunate because, you see, I read about the 4S cheese in *The Cheesemaker's Monthly* and I said to myself, now that would make a good local story, so if you could get Mr or Mrs Kingsley I'd be very grateful. A story like this could make my career."

"They've gone away," Suzanne blurted out. "On a long holiday."

"How long?"

"Oh, a month I believe, they're spending their prize money on a trip to Antarctica, which will take at least a month. I'm just here to keep an eye on the house. I suggest you come back in a month."

"I'll do that. Here is my card, perhaps you could ask them to phone as soon as they get back. Thank you very much for your time."

Suzanne leaned against the door in relief. Oscar seized his moment and raced in. Mum and Dad, Mr Mouse and Katie all raced for the mouse hole with Oscar in pursuit. Suzanne flung herself after Oscar and caught his tail just before he pounced on Katie. Oscar let out a howl of pain and rage. The journalist heard the shriek and looked in through the window just in time to see Mum and Dad and Katie and Mr Mouse scamper into the mouse hole.

"What's going on in there?" he shouted, banging on the window.

Suzanne scrambled to her feet and ran to the door.

"Hi there," she called. "Silly me, I tripped

over the cat. Nothing to worry about."

"Don't give me that. I saw three little people running around that house; there's something odd going on here and I intend getting to the bottom of it."

"Little people, you're seeing things,"

laughed the inspector nervously.

"I know what I saw," snapped the journalist. "I don't have hallucinations and I'm not drunk, what I saw was three tiny people." He shook his head in a puzzled way. "I know it sounds ridiculous but that is what I saw and you know it is. I don't see how I can leave it at that, this has the makings of a great story and I'll be back soon to sort it out."

"Has he gone?" hissed Dad.

"No, he's wondering around the garden looking puzzled. He's coming back, oh dear. No he isn't but he's making a call on his mobile phone and looking very hard at this house."

"Well, first things first, before anything else put Oscar outside," called Dad from the safety of the mouse hole. "We need to make a plan of action in safety."

So Suzanne carried a protesting Oscar to the door and pushed him out.

"We've got to bring Septimouse round quickly, before that journalist comes back," sighed Mum. "Any ideas anyone?"

"Put cold compresses on his head," suggested Suzanne and so they took it in turns to put cold cotton wool on his head.

But nothing happened.

"We'd better call the doctor," decided Dad.

"The doctor, but what will he think?" said Mum.

"We'll just have to hope we can explain and persuade him to be discreet," declared Dad.

"I mean, what choice do we have?"

6

The Doctor Calls

While Suzanne held the phone, Mum spoke to the doctor.

"If you could pay us a home visit, doctor, we would be immensely grateful. No, I'm afraid I can't come into the surgery, just this once you will have to come to us. Thank you, doctor."

"He wasn't at all happy about it," Mum

told the others.

"He'll understand once he sees how things are here," Katie assured her.

"You'll have to answer the door, Suzanne," Dad told her. "We're so grateful to you. How we would have coped without you, I don't know."

When the doctor came, the inspector led him into the front room and there on the coffee table lined up in a row, were Mum, Dad, Katie and Mr Mouse.

"Good lord," said the doctor and he sat down and shook his head and then cleaned his glasses.

"Sorry to give you a shock Dr Livings," began Mum politely, "I realise this must be very odd for you."

"That is a huge understatement," groaned the doctor. "So what exactly is going on here?"

So between them the four told him the whole story from beginning to end.

"That is the craziest story I ever heard," declared the doctor, "but as I'm here I'd better see the patient."

So Septimouse was carried in. The doctor felt the pulse and the head of the mouse and then looked puzzled.

"As far as I can tell he has concussion and I have no idea how long it takes for a mouse to recover from that. Really I have no experience in these matters... I mean he's so

small. I think a vet could be more use."

"I know an excellent vet - Louise Makin," cried Suzanne.

"Then I suggest you call her without delay," said the doctor putting on his coat. "Good luck, and don't worry, I won't say a word. In fact I don't think anyone would believe a word of it if I did. Let me know what happens, I can't wait to hear the outcome."

"Don't worry doctor, we'll keep you posted," they cried. "Byee."

While the inspector phoned the vet, Mum began to cry.

"Don't, love," said Dad. "We'll get this

sorted out."

"I'm beginning to think that we won't and that we'll be small for ever," wept Mum and they sat in a dejected little circle looking at the completely still figure of Septimouse.

When the vet arrived they all cheered up. Louise Makin just loved the story of the mice and the cheese and was thrilled to be able to talk to Mr Mouse.

"What a bonus, all my life I've worked with animals and now I get to talk to one. And what is more I think the whole world should hear about how the wonderful 4S cheese is made."

"Come on," cried Dad. "No one would buy cheese made by mice, we'd be ruined!"

"I disagree. I'm sure Septimouse would become a hero and a national treasure and the cheese would be even more of a best seller."

Septimouse opened one eye.

"Yes, and he would be a personality, his picture would be in every newspaper and he would be on celebrity chat shows on television - he might even get his own television show!"

Septimouse opened the other eye and gave a little moan.

7

Fame at Last

All the mice and the people went silent and stared at the tiny form of Septimouse on his stretcher.

"My boy, my boy Septimouse, he's alive, he's going to be alright," wept Mrs Mouse.

"Septimouse, wake up," shouted Dad. "Quick, get me some ice someone."

After a few ice packs Septimouse opened

both eyes and said, "Where am I? What happened? Who am I?"

"Oh Septimouse, you had a fall, don't you remember?" cried Katie.

"Who are you?" asked the mouse. "And why are you so small?"

"He doesn't remember a thing," sniffed Mum. "We'll never be our normal size again."

There was a terrible silence, broken by Katie.

"Oh poor Septimouse, there he was about to get what he most wanted and be famous and even go on TV and now he's lost his memory. It's so sad."

"Little big person Katie," said a tiny voice, "did you say something about fame and television?"

"Yes, Septimouse."

"Septimouse? Who is this Septimouse? Oh yes, it comes back to me; I am Septimouse and the seventh son of a seventh son and full of magical powers. Oh yes, I have some faint, tiny memories now."

"Septimouse, if you are to go on TV you have to concentrate very hard now," Katie told him, " because big, big person Mum and big, big person Dad and I are now very small. If you can just manage to remember one of your spells and make us the right size again you will get on TV."

"And if I don't, my old friend?"

"Then I don't fancy your chances of becoming very famous at all, Septimouse," Katie informed him in a very serious tone.

"I think I just remember that one little spell," groaned the mouse.

"Oh my poor head, how it hurts. Now let's see:

> "Mum, Dad and Katie, small like mice,
> Turn right back into lice."

"Septimouse!" they all yelled, "what are you trying to do?"

"Oh I got it wrong," sighed the mouse. "Well, don't shout, I feel very fragile. My head aches."

"Tough," snapped Dad. "Now try again Septimouse, and forget about lice. We want to be people again."

"I know, I know," moaned the mouse. "Just give me a minute."

"Get it right this time or I'll let Oscar loose," threatened Dad.

"Mum, Dad, Katie, small like mice,
Be your proper sizes in a trice."

Suddenly they became full sized again and huge cheers went up.

"Thank goodness for that," smiled Mum. "And we did it before that nosy journalist got back."

"I think we're going to have to come clean on what has been going on," declared Dad, "and take the consequences whatever they are. This is all too nerve wracking. When that journalist comes back, we'll just tell it to him like it is."

Just then the bell rang and Mum answered the door. There stood the journalist and a photographer.

"Oh," said the journalist, "I was told you had gone to the Antarctic for a prolonged period."

"It was too cold," Mum told him. "So we came home early."

"Is that the truth?" asked the journalist.

"Well no," replied Mum smiling, "the truth is a much better story. You see this mouse

here with his head in a bandage is the seventh son of a seventh son and has magical powers."

"You're mad," cried the journalist, making for the door.

"No she isn't," called Septimouse. "I am indeed the seventh son of a seventh son, 4S for short, and I do have magical powers."

"The mouse can talk," shrieked the man.

"That is the least of his talents," Dad informed him. "Septimouse can also make cheese and shrink people. When you came earlier we had been shrunk to attend a cheese party in that mouse hole there. Unfortunately Septimouse had a fall and got concussion and could not bring us back to our real sizes until a minute ago."

"You're not having me on?" he asked nervously.

"No really," said Katie, "Septimouse could shrink you too and you could go and see his cheese factory."

"4S cheese, now I understand. Yes, so shrink me. I would love to see the factory, oh what a scoop, I'm made, I'm made."

"Shrink me too," cried the photographer. "This is the best fun."

So the journalist and the photographer were duly shrunk and went to look at the factory. They came out glowing and were made big again.

"Oh, it's lovely in there," smiled the photographer. "It's so clean and cosy."

"What an experience," agreed the journalist. "Just wait till I tell my friends on television. Oh this is so thrilling, I love you Septimouse. Yes, there's a whole TV programme in this and I bet we can get it shown at prime time too. Real family

entertainment. The punters are going to love it."

"So what are you planning?" demanded Septimouse. "I need to know, so that I can fit you into my very busy life."

"I was very much hoping you could fit us in to film tomorrow at around mid-day. Would that suit you, Septimouse?"

"I'll have to consult my diary," commented the mouse and he got out a small black book. "Mid-day you say, no, I can't manage that, but 2 o'clock would be quite convenient."

"No worries," agreed the journalist. "2 o'clock it is. Now make me proper size again, so that I can get it all arranged."

And so it was that the next day a TV crew arrived at 2 p.m.

Septimouse looked at the crew and the cameras.

"You'll all have to be shrunk," he told them.
"And the cameras. Are you all willing?"

"We are," they shouted."More than willing,
we're keen.

So Septimouse shrunk them and the
cameras and they all scurried into the mouse

hole, whooping and dancing. After a minute
Septimouse came out.

"We've decided to have the party for the

cameras, so you all have to be shrunk and come to the party."

"No!' shouted Dad, but it was too late and within seconds they were all shrunk.

"Stop complaining, man," sang Septimouse. "Come on, let's party!"

So they all went into the mouse hole and ate and danced and sang and the TV cameras filmed it all.

Suddenly Septimouse stopped.

"Where's my friend Oscar?" he asked. "I want my dear old friend here for my moment of triumph."

"Oscar's been horrible, he's been chasing us all when we were very small," Katie explained.

"Stop the cameras a minute," Septimouse cried, and he ran to the mouse hole and called, "Oscar, dear friend, what is this I hear about you chasing big, big person Dad and big, big person Mum and poor little big

88

person Katie?"

There was the sound of a cat wailing.

"Oscar says he was hurt because no one invited him to the party, and anyway what do you expect of a cat if no one bothers to feed him?" Septimouse informed them. "And he says it's not his fault he was born a cat and that cats chase little things that move fast, that's just the way it is but he's very sorry and ashamed and wants to be forgiven."

"Well, alright, we do forgive him," said Mum, Dad and Katie. "But be sure there is plenty of food for him."

So Oscar was shrunk and joined in the party and enjoyed himself dancing with Katie.

"Septimouse, make a speech," called one of the cameramen.

"Yes, speech, speech," they all shouted.

"If you insist," replied Septimouse modestly.

"Ladies, gentlemen, mice and cat," he began. "Being a shy and modest kind of a mouse and not at all used to public speaking, I will make this speech short. I just want to say how happy I am that my little cheese is at last getting some recognition and that I am getting the credit I so richly deserve. Now that I no longer have to be a secret but am about to become a great celebrity I want you all to know how lucky you are to have known me, for now Septimouse the Great belongs to the whole world and not just the world of mice and the home of big, big person Mum and big, big person Dad and little big person Katie . My hour has come at last and you are privileged to witness it. I propose a toast to me, to Septimouse."

"To Septimouse," they all said, raising their glasses and trying not to smile.

At that moment Septimouse, with his arm outstretched and raising his glass to himself, began to wobble.

"Watch it," yelled Dad, "don't fall again!" and he managed to grab him - just in the very nick of time.

Septimouse, Supermouse!

Septimouse, Big Cheese!

Meet Septimouse, Supermouse!

He's the seventh son and a truly magical mouse. Septimouse can talk to cats and humans – and he can even make them as tiny as he is.

"These amusing and warmly told books will be much enjoyed"   *Books for Keeps*

"Delicious stories to curl up with"   *The Lady*

Ann Jungman was a teacher before becoming a full-time writer. She is a well known visitor to schools. Her other titles, published by Happy Cat Books, are the *Broomstick* series of books about the witches Mabel, Ethel and their sister Maud - read all about them in *Broomstick Services, Broomstick Removals, Broomstick Rescues* and *Broomstick Baby*.